CALENDAR CLUB MYSTERIES™

The Case of the
BACK·TO·SCHOOL
BURGLAR

CALENDAR CLUB MYSTERIES™

The Case of the
BACK·TO·SCHOOL
BURGLAR

by **NANCY STAR**

Illustrated by
JAMES BERNARDIN

SCHOLASTIC INC.

New York   Toronto   London   Auckland   Sydney
Mexico City   New Delhi   Hong Kong   Buenos Aires

For Emma and Jack
—N. S.

ISBN-13: 978-0-439-91175-7
ISBN-10: 0-439-91175-3

Text copyright © 2005 by Nancy Star.
Illustrations copyright © 2005 by Scholastic Inc.
All rights reserved. Published by Scholastic Inc.

12 11 10 9 8 7 6 5 4 3 2 1   6 7 8 9 10 11/0

Printed in the U.S.A.   40
This edition first printing, September 2006

Book design by Jennifer Rinaldi Windau

CALENDAR CLUB MYSTERIES™

The Case of the
BACK-TO-SCHOOL
BURGLAR

CHAPTER ONE
MISSING PRIZES!

Dottie noticed it first. "The box of prizes!" she said.

She pointed to the empty table. "It's gone!"

"But I just put it there a minute ago," said Leon.

"Then where did it go?" asked Casey.

Best friends Dottie Plum, Casey Calendar, and Leon Spector were spending the morning at Fruitvale Elementary School.

School hadn't officially started yet. But tomorrow was the annual Back-to-School Carnival. And there was still a lot to do.

Most of the volunteers were setting up carnival booths in the gym.

Dottie, Casey, and Leon were sorting prizes for the Prize Room.

"That box had twenty-five giant magnifying glasses in it," Leon said. "I was hoping to win one of them."

"I was hoping for a beanbag dog," Dottie said. "There were twenty-five beanbag dogs in there, too."

"Where do you think the box could be?" Casey asked.

"Maybe someone put the prizes away for us," Dottie said.

"Come on," Casey said. "Let's go look."

They rushed into the Prize Room. It was really the nurse's office.

The nurse had let Dottie, Casey, and Leon take all the Band-Aids and tissue boxes off her shelves. Now the shelves held magnet sets, bouncy balls, modeling clay packs, and butterfly nets.

But there were no beanbag dogs or

Carnival Prizes
Model Clay Packs
Butterfly Nets
Bouncy Balls
Bean Bags
Magnifyi

magnifying glasses.

"Maybe someone moved the box to the gym by mistake," Dottie said.

"Come on," Casey said. "Let's go see."

They were halfway to the gym when Leon stopped.

"Look," he said. He pointed to the wall. "That's where we put the Lollipop Tree! Now it's gone!"

The cardboard Lollipop Tree was a carnival favorite. Lollipops were taped to all its branches. Every lollipop had a number on it that matched a prize. So everyone who picked a lollipop got a prize, and they got to keep the lollipop, too!

"Who would take the Lollipop Tree?" Casey asked. "Do you think someone moved that to the gym, also?"

They hurried to find out.

The first person they saw in the gym was Dottie's mother. She was setting up bowling pins in one of the booths.

"Hi, Mrs. Plum," called Casey. "Did you see the Lollipop Tree?"

"Isn't it in the hall?" asked Mrs. Plum. She turned and knocked down all the bowling pins. She laughed and started to set them up again.

They saw Leon's father next. He was emptying a large bag of sand into a big plastic sandbox for the Dinosaur Dig.

"Have you seen any magnifying glasses?" Leon asked.

"No," said Mr. Spector. "Just dinosaurs." He buried a bunch of plastic dinosaurs in the sand.

The three friends continued searching the room.

They stopped at the popcorn machine.

Mrs. List was in charge of the snack machines. She was their neighbor. She was also a kindergarten teacher at the school.

5

"I'm testing the machines to make sure they work," Mrs. List explained.

"Do you need any help tasting the popcorn?" Casey asked.

Mrs. List laughed. "Maybe later," she said.

"Do you need help tasting sno-cones?" Casey asked.

"I've already tested that machine," Mrs. List said. "It works perfectly."

"I love sno-cones and popcorn," Leon said.

"This is going to be the best carnival ever," Dottie said. "If we find those missing prizes and the tree."

The three friends searched the rest of the gym and the classrooms. But they couldn't find the Lollipop Tree or the missing box of prizes anywhere.

They were on their way back to the Prize Room when they saw a girl holding a large sign. The sign said FERRIS WHEEL.

"Did the carnival man bring his Ferris

wheel?" Casey asked.

The girl nodded. She had big brown eyes and a friendly smile.

"I just made this sign," she said. "Do you like it?" She looked proud of her work.

"Yes," Casey said. "What's your name?"

"Victoria," the girl said. "Do you want to see the Ferris wheel? It's behind the school, next to the pony."

"The pony's here?" Casey said. "I love ponies!"

"Me, too!" Dottie said. "Let's go see it."

Victoria watched as the three friends ran outside.

"The Ferris wheel is my favorite," Leon said.

"What about the Pie Toss contest?" Casey asked. "I thought that was your favorite."

Casey's mom made the whipped-cream pies for the Pie Toss contest. Mrs. Calendar owned Sweetie Pie, Fruitvale's favorite bakery. And everyone agreed — she made the best cakes, chocolate chip brownies, and whipped-cream pies in the world.

"The Pie Toss is my other favorite," Leon said.

The Pie Toss was the last event of the carnival. The winner got to toss a pie at a mystery guest. The guest was a mystery because the pie-tosser wore a blindfold.

"Remember when Warren Bunn won the Pie Toss contest last year?" Casey asked.

Warren was a boy in their grade who was a bully and proud of it.

"Are you talking about me?" someone called out.

They turned. Warren was standing with his best friend, Derek Fleck.

"We were talking about the Pie Toss

contest you won," Leon said.

"I wouldn't have thrown the pie so hard if I knew the mystery guest was the principal," Warren said. He glared at Derek. "Nobody warned me."

Warren was still mad at Derek about it.

"Dumb Pie Toss," he muttered. He pushed his way past them and walked into the school.

"Dumb carnival," Derek said. He followed his friend inside.

Dottie, Casey, and Leon tried not to laugh. But it was hard. Principal Elder had looked very funny with whipped cream all over his face.

"I wouldn't mind being the mystery guest," Dottie said. "I love whipped-cream pies."

"I hope the pies aren't missing," Leon said.

"Do you think someone took them?"

Casey asked. "Let's go check."

They hurried to the school cafeteria. They had put the pies in the large refrigerator that morning.

Casey opened the refrigerator door.

"They're gone!" Dottie said.

They stared at the empty shelves.

"Why would someone steal our pies, the prizes, and the Lollipop Tree?" Casey asked.

"Come on," Dottie said. "This calls for a special meeting of the Calendar Club."

CHAPTER TWO

A NOTE!

The Calendar Club was famous in Fruitvale for solving mysteries. Dottie, Casey, and Leon were its first and only members.

They hurried to Daisy Lane and raced up Casey's driveway. The clubhouse was in her backyard.

Dottie went inside first. She loved to be first, and all her friends knew it.

Casey stopped at the Help Box. The Help Box was where anyone in Fruitvale could leave a note about a problem.

Dottie, Casey, and Leon took turns checking the box every day. Today was Casey's turn.

But Casey didn't look inside the box. She

picked it up and carried it into the clubhouse. She put it down in the middle of the floor.

"I'm glad we decided to fill up the Help Box with jelly beans for the 'Guess How Many?' Jelly Beans contest," Casey said.

"Me, too," Dottie said.

"Do you think everyone will notice the jelly bean box is really our Help Box?" Casey asked.

"Yes," Dottie said. "And I think the Help Box will remind everyone that the Calendar Club is always ready to help."

"Did you know Mr. Cliff donated a fish tank and five goldfish for whoever guesses the right number of jelly beans?" Casey asked.

Mr. Cliff owned Pet Me, a pet store next to Mrs. Calendar's bakery.

Dottie nodded. "He also donated a year's supply of fish food. Now all we need are the jelly beans."

"Leon, did you get the jelly beans yet?"

Casey asked.

Leon didn't answer.

"Leon?" Casey asked again. She looked around.

The clubhouse wasn't that big. It didn't take long to figure out that Leon was nowhere to be seen.

This was nothing new.

"Leon!" Dottie and Casey shouted.

They looked at each other and shrugged. They knew Leon would show up eventually.

"Eventually" meant Leon would show up after he checked every pile of leaves, gravel, and dirt that he passed.

Leon was a collector. His most important collection was of rocks in the shape of states. Leon was trying to make an entire map of the United States out of rocks.

But looking for rocks in the shape of states took a lot of time. That was why

Leon was almost always late.

Leon burst through the door. He was out of breath. He had been running.

"Did you find something?" Casey asked.

"Just a rock that looks like Texas," Leon said.

"Don't you already have a rock that looks like Texas?" Casey asked.

Leon nodded. "I don't understand why I keep finding the states I already have," he said, "and not the states I really need."

Leon noticed the Help Box in the middle of the floor. He peered through the slot.

"Were you waiting for me before you took out the note?" he asked.

"Is there a note in the box?" Casey asked. "Was it there the whole time?"

Casey always asked a lot of questions. But her friends were used to it.

"It's your turn to read it," Dottie told Casey.

Casey took the note out of the box.

Dottie took her notebook out of her back pocket. She carried the notebook wherever she went. Inside she kept lists. Her favorite list was of the weather.

Today, her weather list said, is seventy degrees with big puffy clouds in the sky.

She turned to a new page and wrote: "Help Box Note."

Casey read the note out loud while Dottie copied it down.

"Dear Calendar Club,

Are you missing a tree with lollipops on it?

Look in the bushes near the side door to the school."

"Who is it from?" Leon asked.

"It's signed, 'A friend,'" Casey said. "Do you think it's true?" she asked. "Do you think the Lollipop Tree is in the bushes outside of school?"

"I think there's only one way to find out," Dottie said.

CHAPTER THREE

LOST AND FOUND!

Dottie got to school first.

Casey was right behind her.

Leon, as always, came last.

"There," said Dottie. She pointed to the tree. It was partly hidden in the bushes.

They moved closer to examine it.

"Look!" Leon said. "Some of the lollipops are gone."

Dottie counted. "Ten of them are gone!"

"Did they fall off?" Casey asked.

Leon walked over to the bushes to see if any were on the ground.

Dottie took out her notebook. She turned to a page called Lollipop Tree.

"We put red, orange, purple, and yellow lollipops on the tree," Dottie said. "But only red ones are missing."

"Why would only red ones fall off?" Casey asked.

"Maybe someone took them off," Dottie said. She held open the door to the school.

Casey carried the Lollipop Tree inside. She placed it back where it belonged.

"It's a good thing you saw the note in the Help Box, Leon," Dottie said.

Leon didn't answer.

"Leon?" Dottie called.

Leon was nowhere to be seen.

Dottie and Casey found him outside, still examining the dirt.

He opened his hand and showed them a rock.

"Texas again," Leon said.

He put the rock down just as Warren and Derek came running out of the school.

They were laughing hard. They stopped

when they saw Leon.

"Hey, Rock-Head," Warren said. "Did you find something important?"

His question made Casey suspicious.

"What do you mean?" she asked.

"What do you think I mean?" said Warren. "I mean did Rock-Head discover another dumb rock nobody cares about?"

"Yeah, Leon," said Derek. "I heard you found one that looks like a lollipop."

Casey narrowed her eyes. She walked over to Derek.

"Why are your lips so red?" Casey asked.

"They're not red," Derek said. He quickly wiped his lips on his sleeve.

"What's that?" Casey pointed at the red mark where Derek had just wiped his lips.

"Did you eat a red lollipop?" Casey asked.

Warren laughed. "We don't eat lollipops."

"Lollipops are for babies," Derek said.

"Itty-bitty babies and loco-poco rock collectors with freckles all over their faces," Warren said.

Derek laughed so hard he fell to the ground.

Leon got mad. Leon had freckles all over his face. His mother said his freckles gave him personality. She said one day he'd be glad he had freckles. But so far that hadn't happened yet.

Mrs. Bunn walked out of the school.

"Warren," she called. "You and Derek are supposed to be filling up water balloons." Mrs. Bunn looked at him strangely. "Warren, why are your lips so red?"

Warren turned and smiled at Casey.

"Lollipops," he said.

Then he and Derek followed his mother into the school.

"I think it's time to start a suspect list," Dottie told her friends.

She opened her notebook and wrote down:

Carnival Burglar Suspects:
Number One, Warren Bunn.
Number Two, Derek Fleck.

Just then, a man ran by. "Where are you?" he yelled at someone they couldn't see.

Their mouths dropped open in surprise. The man was running on stilts!

"I've never seen anyone run on stilts before," Leon said.

"I've never seen anyone on stilts except at the circus," Dottie said.

"Who is he?" Casey asked.

Before her friends could answer, Casey raced over to find out.

CHAPTER FOUR
THE CARNIVAL MAN

"Hi," Casey shouted up at the man, just as Dottie and Leon caught up to her.

"That's my name," the man said. "Don't wear it out. And don't shout. I'm not deaf."

"I didn't think you were deaf," Casey said. "I was just saying 'Hi.'"

"That's my name. Hy. Starts with an *H* and ends with a *Y*. And don't ask me why," said Hy.

He sounded annoyed. Casey didn't want to ask him anything.

"You don't remember who I am, do you?" Hy asked.

Casey shook her head.

"I'm the carnival man," Hy said.

"Remember me? I remember you. You're one of the kids who kept asking me to make more balloon animals last year. Remember now?"

Casey didn't remember that at all. But she decided not to say so.

"Last year my balloon clown quit the day before the carnival," Hy said. "This year my stilts walker quit. Do you know how hard it is to run a carnival when you're on stilts?"

The three friends didn't answer because they had no idea.

"Now my kid is hiding from me," Hy complained. "Did you ever try to run a carnival when your kid is hiding from you?"

Dottie, Casey, and Leon had never done that, either. So they stayed silent again.

"What's wrong with you three?" Hy asked. "Did you forget how to talk? You have marshmallows in your ears? You have

lollipops on your brains?"

"Lollipops!" Dottie repeated.

"Did you know someone took our Lollipop Tree?" Casey asked.

"Lollipop Tree? I don't have a stilts walker," Hy said. "And my kid is hiding from me. Why would I care about a bunch of red lollipops?"

Hy turned. He took off in long strides toward the carnival trailer in the parking lot.

"We never said the lollipops were red," Leon whispered.

"Do you think Hy took them?" Casey asked.

"I don't know," Dottie said. "But I'm going to put him on my list."

Dottie added the carnival man to her suspect list. She put her notebook back in her pocket.

Leon's mother came walking toward them.

"Here you are," said Mrs. Spector. "I've

been looking for you. Did you fill up the Help Box with jelly beans yet?"

"We're going to do that right now, aren't we?" Casey asked.

"Yes," Leon said. "Bye, Mom," he called to Mrs. Spector.

And they hurried back to Daisy Lane.

They talked about the case as they walked.

"I don't understand why anyone would want to ruin a carnival," Dottie said. "Carnivals are so much fun."

"It wasn't fun for Warren Bunn last year," Leon said.

"That's true," Dottie agreed. "He's still mad about the Pie Toss contest."

"And anything that makes Warren mad makes Derek mad," added Leon.

"What about the carnival man?" Casey asked. "Why would he want to ruin the carnival?"

"Maybe because his clowns keep

quitting," Leon said.

"Maybe because his kid keeps hiding," Dottie said.

They stopped in front of Leon's house.

"I'll go get the jelly beans," Leon said. He went into his house to find them.

"I'll go get supplies for the 'Guess How Many?' Jelly Beans sign," Casey said. She went into her house to find paper and paint.

"I'll go get Ginger," Dottie said to herself. She went into her house to find her cat.

Ginger was a cat who thought she was a dog. Ginger loved to go for long walks on a leash.

Casey's dog, Silky, thought he was a cat. Silky liked to spend all day in front of the dining room window, watching the world go by.

Leon didn't have a pet. He had allergies. So he collected rocks instead.

Dottie and Ginger got to the clubhouse first. Casey came next.

Leon, as always, came last.

He carried three big bags of jelly beans. He put them on the floor.

Casey noticed that one of his pockets looked full.

"Did you find a state?" she asked.

"I found something," Leon said. He took a rock out of his pocket.

"Is it Florida?" Casey asked.

Leon had been looking for Florida ever since his grandparents moved there.

He put the rock on the floor. "No," he said. He studied it for a moment. "It's not Iowa or Wisconsin, either."

"I didn't know you were looking for Iowa and Wisconsin," Dottie said.

"I wasn't," Leon said. "Until Hy mentioned balloon animals. That reminded me about the National Balloon Museum in Iowa."

Leon knew a lot of facts like that. But Dottie and Casey didn't mind. They were used to it.

"I started thinking about Wisconsin because of the stilts," he said. "Stilts made me think of the circus. Wisconsin has a great circus museum."

"Is there a state with a Museum of Lost Whipped-Cream Pies?" Casey asked. "Because if there is, could we go there?"

Leon knew Casey wasn't serious.

He walked over to the Help Box.

"We got another one," he said.

"Another note?" Casey asked.

She lifted up the lid of the box and pulled out a note. She gave it to Leon. It was his turn to read it out loud.

"Dear Calendar Club,

Are you missing a box of prizes? Did you know that a criminal always returns to the scene of the crime?

From,

A Friend."

"Who is leaving us notes?" Casey asked. "And what does it mean?"

"I don't know who left the note," Dottie said. "But I do know where the scene of the crime is. Everything missing was taken at school."

"Then we need to go back to school," Leon said.

"First we have to fill up the Help Box with jelly beans," Dottie said.

Casey and Leon agreed.

Leon emptied the bags of jelly beans into the Help Box.

Dottie wrote down exactly how many jelly beans were in each bag.

Casey made the "Guess How Many?" Jelly Beans sign.

They carried the box and the sign to Casey's red wagon. Ginger hopped in and they hurried back to the scene of the crime.

CHAPTER FIVE
THE SCENE OF THE CRIME

The Help Box was filled to the top with jelly beans. Leon put it on a table in front of the gym. Casey opened the lid so people could see inside. Dottie put the "Guess How Many?" Jelly Beans sign next to it.

"Now, where exactly is the scene of the crime?" Casey asked.

Leon pointed to the Prize Room. "I think it's over there," he said.

Officer Gill was standing outside the Prize Room door. He was talking to someone. And he looked worried.

"Come on," Casey said. "Let's go see what's wrong."

Officer Gill smiled when he saw them coming.

"Here come my favorite detectives!" he said. "Solve any crimes today? I hope not. Not on the day before the carnival!"

"We didn't solve any crimes. But we think — " Dottie stopped herself.

The carnival man stepped out of the Prize Room. She didn't want to talk to Officer Gill in front of him.

Officer Gill could tell Dottie was upset.

"Will you excuse us for a moment?" he asked Hy. "The Calendar Club and I have something to discuss."

Hy scowled. He walked down the hall and into the gym.

"Is something wrong?" asked Officer Gill.

"Yes," said Dottie. "Someone is taking things."

"Did you hear what happened to our Lollipop Tree?" Casey asked. "And the box of beanbag dogs and magnifying glasses? And the whipped-cream pies? And do you

33

think the thief always returns to the scene of the crime?"

"Slow down," said Officer Gill. He took his notebook out of his back pocket. "Let's start with the Lollipop Tree. What happened to it?"

Dottie took her notebook out of her pocket. "It was stolen," she said.

Officer Gill scratched his head. "I thought I just saw it."

"That's because we found it," Leon said.

"But the whipped-cream pies are still gone," Dottie said.

"We put them in the refrigerator this morning and they disappeared," Leon said.

"Whipped-cream pies have a habit of disappearing," said Officer Gill, but he wrote it down, anyway.

"But boxes of carnival prizes don't just disappear," Dottie said.

"Carnival prizes disappeared?" asked

Officer Gill.

Dottie nodded. "Good ones. Beanbag dogs and magnifying glasses!"

Officer Gill looked at the table in front of the Prize Room. There was a box in the middle of the table.

He reached in the box and lifted out a large plastic bag. It was filled with giant magnifying glasses. He lifted out another large bag. It was filled with beanbag dogs.

"Are these the missing prizes?" asked Officer Gill.

"Yes!" the three friends said together.

"Looks like someone found them and

returned them," said Officer Gill. "I guess the problem is solved."

"The problem isn't solved," Dottie said.

"Someone took the Lollipop Tree and dumped it in the bushes," Leon said.

"And this prize box was missing for awhile," Dottie said.

"And the whipped-cream pies are still missing," Casey said. "Don't you see? Someone is trying to ruin our carnival."

"I think you should talk to the principal about this," said Officer Gill. "It sounds like something Mr. Elder would want to know."

"That's a very good idea," Dottie said.

"Thank you," said Officer Gill.

The three friends hurried down the hall to Principal Elder's office.

Leon stopped as they passed the gym.

"Wait!" he called to his friends. "Look!"

Dottie and Casey came back and looked.

The "Guess How Many?" Jelly Beans sign was on the table in front of the gym exactly where they put it.

But the Calendar Club Help Box was gone!

CHAPTER SIX
FOLLOWING THE TRACKS

"How could someone take our Help Box?" Casey asked.

"We'd better tell Officer Gill and Mr. Elder," Dottie said.

They couldn't find Officer Gill anywhere. And the principal wasn't in his office.

"Maybe they're outside," Dottie said.

They walked outside to look.

Casey stopped at the bottom of the steps.

"Where's my wagon?" she asked.

They had parked her red wagon in the dirt next to the school steps. Now the wagon was gone, too.

"The jelly beans made the Help Box heavy," Dottie said. "Maybe someone used the wagon to take it away."

Leon pointed to the ground. "Look! Tire tracks."

"Come on," Casey said. "Let's see where they go."

They followed the tracks. Leon stopped several times to pick up things from the ground.

"Leon," Dottie called to him. "This isn't a good time to look for rocks."

But Leon didn't listen. His friends walked on ahead. He stopped to pick things up.

He caught up to Dottie, Ginger, and Casey at the school playground. They didn't look happy.

"We can't find any more tracks," Dottie said.

Leon looked around. "There it is!" he said. He pointed.

Dottie and Casey saw the wagon, too. It was parked under the slide.

They ran to look inside.

"Empty," Dottie said when they got there. "Our Help Box is gone."

"How can people leave us notes if we don't have a Help Box anymore?" Casey asked.

"We have to find it," Dottie said.

"It's over there," Leon said. He pointed toward the parking lot.

"How do you know?" Casey asked.

Leon didn't answer. He walked a few more steps. He bent down and picked something up. He ran ahead. He stopped again.

Dottie and Casey weren't used to Leon leading the way.

They ran and caught up to him.

"What are you doing?" Casey said in a loud voice.

Leon put his finger to his lips so she'd be quiet.

Dottie and Casey saw why. They had run all the way to the carnival trailer. A strange sound came from inside.

"I think someone's crying," Dottie whispered.

The trailer door swung open.

"What are you doing here?" Hy asked. His cheeks were red. He looked embarrassed.

"We're looking for a box with jelly beans in it," Casey said. "It disappeared. It's really important to us."

"Well, I can't help you," Hy said.

The crying got louder.

"Can't you hear I've got an upset kid?" asked Hy. "Why are you still here?"

"We're not," Casey said.

They turned and ran away as fast as they could.

CHAPTER SEVEN

VICTORIA'S OFFER

They stopped running when they got to the front of the school. They sat down on the steps to catch their breath.

They were still sitting there when a girl walked by.

"You're Victoria, right?" Casey asked. "The girl who made the Ferris wheel sign."

Victoria nodded. She sniffled. She looked as if she'd been crying.

"Are you okay?" asked Casey.

Victoria nodded. "I'm fine," she said. She smiled to prove it.

"I'm Casey," Casey said. "This is Dottie and Leon."

"I know," Victoria said.

"You know us?" Casey asked.

Victoria nodded again. "I came to the

carnival last year, too." She leaned closer and whispered. "Did you get my notes?"

The three friends exchanged glances.

"I left you notes in your Help Box," Victoria said. "Did you get them?"

"They were from you?" Casey asked.

Victoria nodded.

"How did you know we had a Help Box?" Casey asked.

"Everyone knows about the Calendar Club Help Box," Victoria said.

"I have another note," she said. "But I don't know where to put it now that your box is missing."

"How do you know our box is missing?" Casey asked. "Did you see someone take it?"

Victoria didn't answer. She reached into her pocket and took out her note. "I'll just read it to you," she said. She read the note out loud.

Dear Calendar Club,

Will you let me be in your club if I find your Help Box?

She handed the note to Casey.

"I'm very good at figuring things out," Victoria said.

"What do you think? Will you let me join your club if I find your box?"

The three friends looked at one another and shrugged.

"Okay," Leon said.

Victoria clapped her hands. "I can't wait! What's the secret password?"

"We don't have a secret password," Dottie said.

"What's the special knock to get into the clubhouse?" Victoria asked.

"We don't have a special knock," Leon said.

"When is the secret ceremony?" Victoria asked.

"What secret ceremony?" Casey asked.

"You know," Victoria said. She sounded annoyed. "The special thing you do when you let someone in your club. When is that?"

"We don't have anything like that," Leon said.

"What do you have?" Victoria asked. "Do you have a special membership card?"

"No," Dottie said. "We just have a club."

"How can it be a club if you don't have a password or a membership card?" Victoria asked. "If you don't have a special knock, anyone who wants to can come right into your clubhouse."

"Anyone who wants to *can* come right into our clubhouse," Dottie said.

"Most people don't because they're too busy," Leon said. "Most people play soccer or take piano lessons or go to art class."

"We just solve mysteries," Dottie explained.

"I changed my mind," Victoria said. "I don't want to be in your dumb club if just anyone can join."

"Okay," Dottie said.

"Do you know where our Help Box is?" Casey asked.

"I might," Victoria said. "And then again, I might not."

CHAPTER EIGHT
RED LICORICE

Just then, the principal's car pulled up in front of the school.

Mr. Elder got out. He carried a big shopping bag.

"Good morning, everyone," said Mr. Elder.

"Good morning, Mr. Elder," said Victoria sweetly. "How are you today?"

"I'm fine, Victoria," said the principal.

The three friends were surprised Victoria and Mr. Elder knew each other.

"How are you feeling today?" he asked her.

"The usual," said Victoria.

Dottie, Casey, and Leon suddenly noticed that Victoria looked very sad.

Mr. Elder looked sad, too. "I know what will cheer you up," he said.

He reached into his bag. "I have some

extra packets of prize candy. Would you like one?"

Victoria nodded quickly.

Mr. Elder pulled out a small paper bag and gave it to her.

Victoria held the bag close to her. She looked worried that someone might take it.

"That one is just for you," said Mr. Elder.

"Thank you," said Victoria.

Mr. Elder turned to Dottie, Casey, and Leon.

"Would you like some, too?" He pulled out three more packets.

"Thank you for being such great helpers at the carnival," said Mr. Elder. He handed them each a packet.

Victoria scowled and ran away.

"You'll have to forgive her," Mr. Elder said. "Victoria doesn't get to play with other children very often."

"Why not?" Casey asked. "Who does

she play with?"

"Her father and mother, mostly," said the principal. "And maybe a few clowns from time to time."

"Why does she play with clowns?" Casey asked.

"Her father is the carnival man," said Mr. Elder. "Didn't you know that?"

Dottie, Casey, and Leon shook their heads. They had no idea.

"Victoria wants to go to a school like ours," said Mr. Elder. "But her family moves around too much. So she can't. That's why she's so lonely. And that's why I was so happy to see you talking to her. She can really use some friends."

"Hey," Victoria called. She ran back toward them.

"She really likes you," said Mr. Elder. "That's nice to see." He smiled and went into the school.

Victoria ran up to Dottie. "What color candy did you get?" she asked. "Did you get red or black?"

Dottie looked in her bag. "I got black licorice," she said.

Casey looked into her bag. "I got black, too," she said.

Leon looked in his bag. "I got red licorice."

"You have to switch with me," Victoria said to him.

"Why?" Leon asked.

Victoria didn't feel like explaining. She pulled Leon's bag out of his hand and dropped her own bag on the ground.

She stuck a red licorice stick in her mouth. "Thanks," she said.

She skipped away with the rest of Leon's candy.

Leon picked up the bag Victoria dropped.

"What was that all about?" Casey asked.

Leon stared into the bag. He was thinking so hard it was as if he didn't hear her.

Dottie picked up a small rock.

"Look, Leon," she said, to get his attention. "I think this rock looks like Wisconsin." She handed him the rock.

Leon put it in his pocket without looking at it.

"Leon," Casey said. "What's wrong?"

Leon looked up. "I think I figured out who's been trying to ruin the carnival. And I don't think it's Hy."

He was about to explain. But Warren and Derek came running out of the school.

The bullies ran past them and around to the back of the building.

Mrs. Bunn ran out a moment later.

"Warren," she yelled. "I know you're out here. I'm very angry with you. Mrs. List just told me you've been sneaking off with red sno-cones." She noticed the three friends. "Did Warren run behind the school?"

They nodded.

"Warren Bunn," she called. She marched away to find him.

"If Warren stole red sno-cones do you think he's the one who took the red lollipops?" Casey asked. "Do you think he took the prize box and the Help Box and the whipped-cream pies?"

"No. I think— " Leon stopped talking.

Mrs. Bunn marched back pulling Warren by the hand. Derek trailed behind them.

"I think we should talk somewhere else," Leon said quietly.

"Come on," Casey said. "Let's go to the clubhouse. You can tell us there."

CHAPTER NINE
RED JELLY BEANS

Leon sat down as soon as they were inside the clubhouse. He emptied his pockets and put what was in them on the floor.

"Jelly beans!" Dottie said.

"Where did you get all of them?" Casey asked.

"I found them at school," Leon said. "In the playground, on the driveway, and in the parking lot."

Dottie counted. "You found twenty-two jelly beans."

"Twenty-two black jelly beans," Leon said. "From our Help Box."

"How do you know they're from our box?" Casey asked.

"Because these jelly beans led me to

your wagon," Leon said.

"Is this what you were picking up all that time?" Casey asked. "Not rocks?"

"Not rocks," Leon said.

"Why would someone throw jelly beans on the ground?" Casey asked.

Dottie opened her notebook and turned to a page called Facts About Jelly Beans.

"We put purple, yellow, black, pink, and red jelly beans in the Help Box," Dottie said.

"How come you only found black ones on the ground?" Casey asked.

"Because the person who took the Help Box doesn't like black jelly beans," Leon said.

"I love black jelly beans," Dottie said. "They taste like black licorice."

"I love black licorice," Casey said.

"Victoria doesn't," Leon said. "That's why she took my red licorice. Do you want

to guess her favorite lollipop color?" he
asked.

"Red?" Casey asked.

Leon nodded.

"Do you think Victoria took everything?"
Casey asked.

"I think so," Leon said. "But I'm not
completely sure."

"I have an idea," Casey said. She stood up.

"Wait," Dottie said. She heard
something. She pointed to the door.

"Is someone outside?" Casey whispered.

Leon tiptoed to the clubhouse door. He
peeked outside.

"I heard something, too," Leon said.
"But I don't see anyone."

They all moved close together in case
someone was hiding outside and listening in.

Casey cupped her hands over her mouth.
She whispered the plan.

CHAPTER TEN

THE PLAN

They worked hard for the rest of the afternoon.

Dottie designed the Calendar Club Badge.

Leon made up the secret password.

Casey figured out the special knock.

Together they worked on the secret ceremony.

They returned to school as soon as they were finished.

They found Victoria sitting on a crate next to the Ferris wheel. Next to her were three whipped-cream pies.

"Are those ours?" Casey asked.

Victoria stood up. "I just found them," she said. "I was just going to bring them back to school. What do you want, anyway?"

"We came to ask if you want to learn the special knock," Leon said. "If you still want to join our club."

"We'll teach you the password, too," Dottie said. "I have your membership card." She held it up.

"Do you still want to join?" Casey asked.

"I do," Victoria said. "I really, really do."

"Then let's go," Casey said. "We can have our meeting inside school."

Dottie, Casey, and Leon carried the whipped-cream pies.

Victoria followed them into the school.

Dottie led the way. She stopped when they got to the Prize Room.

"This is a good spot," she said. She sat down on the floor.

Casey and Leon sat beside her.

"Shouldn't we go somewhere private?" Victoria asked. "Like the clubhouse?"

"This is a perfect place," Dottie said. "Unless you don't want to join."

"I want to join," Victoria said. She sat down next to Casey.

Leon explained the secret ceremony. "We'll each ask the person next to us a question," he said. "It can be any question at all."

"But you have to answer honestly," Dottie said.

"Because if anyone thinks you're not being honest, you can't be in the club. Do you understand?" Casey asked.

"Yes," Victoria said.

"I'll go first," Dottie said. She turned to Leon. "Do you really think you're going to be able to find a rock for every state?"

"Yes," Leon said. "I really do."

"I believe you," Dottie said.

"So do I," Casey said.

"Me, too," Victoria said.

"I'll go next," Leon said. He turned to Casey. "Do you really think your mother's chocolate chip brownies are the best in the whole world?"

"They are the best in the whole world," Casey said. "At least I think so."

"I believe you," Leon said.

"Me, too," Victoria said.

"My turn," Casey said. She turned to Victoria. "Are you the one who stole our Help Box and the Lollipop Tree and the box of prizes?"

Victoria looked at the floor.

"You have to be honest," Dottie reminded her.

"Yes," Victoria admitted. "I stole them."

"Were you eavesdropping on us in the clubhouse?" Casey asked.

Victoria nodded.

"Why?" Casey asked.

"I'm really sorry," Victoria said. "I wanted to be in the Calendar Club so much. I thought if I helped you solve a mystery you would let me in."

"You stole all those things just so you could help us find them?" Casey asked.

Victoria nodded. "I guess it was a bad idea. I guess I'm not going to be in your club after all, am I?"

"I guess not," Leon said.

"Wait here," said Victoria. "I'll get your Help Box."

She stood up. "I'm really sorry," she said. Then she ran outside.

Dottie, Casey, and Leon waited right where they were.

Victoria walked back into the school just as Mr. Elder walked out of his office.

He saw her carrying the heavy Help Box. He smiled.

"It's so nice to see you being so helpful," said Mr. Elder. "Don't you think Victoria is a great help?" he asked Dottie, Casey, and Leon.

Victoria looked very sad. She waited for the three friends to tell on her.

Casey stood up. She walked over to Victoria and took the box.

"Thank you," was all Casey said.

And the three friends walked away without another word.

CHAPTER ELEVEN
CARNIVAL DAY!

The carnival was set to start at nine o'clock in the morning.

Dottie, Casey, and Leon got to school half an hour early.

The first grown-up they saw at school was Officer Gill. He was working with Dottie's brother, Jack, to set up the Pie Toss station.

"Do you have time to talk to us?" Casey asked Officer Gill.

Officer Gill always had time to talk to the Calendar Club.

They sat down together. The three friends told him what happened.

"Victoria seems so unhappy," Leon said.

"We want to help her," Casey said. "But we're not sure how."

"We wanted to tell you," Dottie said. "But we don't want Victoria to get in trouble."

"You don't have to worry about that," said Officer Gill. "In fact, don't worry about anything. Today is the Back-to-School Carnival. It's a day to have fun."

Mr. Elder came outside to ring a big bell. The carnival started.

Dottie, Casey, and Leon tried to have fun. They did a pretty good job.

Leon won prize tickets at the Dinosaur Dig. He exchanged them for a giant magnifying glass.

Dottie knocked down all the pins at the bowling booth. She turned her tickets in for a beanbag dog.

Casey popped the most water balloons of anyone all day. She picked a butterfly net and modeling clay for prizes.

They got the last three lollipops from the

Lollipop Tree. They picked their numbers for the Pie Toss contest. Then they stopped for snacks.

Warren Bunn was handing out sno-cones. He had to work for Mrs. List all day long.

Dottie, Casey, and Leon decided to skip the sno-cones. They got cotton candy instead.

They went outside and sat on a bench to eat.

Hy walked by on his stilts.

"Hey," he called to them. "I need to talk to you."

"Uh-oh," Leon said.

Hy got off his stilts and sat down next to them.

"We didn't want to get Victoria in trouble," Dottie said. "We're sorry."

"You've got nothing to be sorry for," said Hy. "I'm the one who's sorry. I've been a terrible grouch. I guess I didn't realize how worried I was about Victoria."

"Is she going to be okay?" asked Casey.

"Yes," said Hy. "We had a long talk with Officer Gill this morning. Victoria's mother and I decided it's time to get a house and settle down. I'll still have to travel now and then. But Victoria doesn't have to come along. She wants to go to a regular school like yours. I guess she's been trying to tell us that for some time. Lucky for her, this time the Calendar Club was listening."

"Is she going to our school?" Casey asked.

"I'm not sure," said Hy. "But if she doesn't go here, it will be somewhere close by."

"Close enough so we can visit?" Casey asked.

"That would be great," said Hy.

"Attention," a voice called over the loudspeaker. It was Mr. Elder.

"All students and families, please check your tickets for the Pie Toss contest. The winning number is 3-8-4-2."

"That's me!" Victoria ran over from the playground. She jumped up and down. "It's me! It's my number!"

Mr. Elder escorted Victoria to the Pie Toss station. Everyone gathered around.

Victoria closed her eyes. Mr. Elder put on her blindfold.

"Will the mystery guest please come out?" he called.

The mystery guest appeared. Everyone screamed and clapped—except Victoria. She couldn't see that the mystery guest was Officer Gill.

"Don't worry," Dottie told her. "The mystery guest is really nice."

"Throw the pie as hard as you can," Warren shouted.

"Hush, Warren," said Mrs. Bunn.

Victoria threw the pie. She pulled off her blindfold.

She laughed hard when she saw Officer Gill with whipped cream on his nose.

"The pie tastes very good, Mrs. Calendar," Officer Gill called to Casey's mother.

"Thank you," Casey's mother called back.

Everyone waited to find out the winner of the last event — the "Guess How Many?" Jelly Beans contest.

Victoria walked over to wait with her father.

Dottie, Casey, and Leon stood nearby.

"Did you hear the good news?" she asked them. "We're going to get a house. And I'm going to a real school."

The three friends smiled. Hy smiled, too.

Mr. Cliff walked over to the microphone. "The winner of the jelly bean contest," he announced, "is Emma Bunn!"

Warren's little sister squealed with delight.

Mr. Cliff presented Emma with a huge

fish tank.

"That's not fair," whined Warren.
"Emma doesn't even like fish."

"I do, too," Emma insisted.

Everyone laughed.
The carnival was
officially over.

But the fun hadn't
ended for Leon. He felt
something in his pocket. He took it out and
smiled.

"What is it?" Casey asked.

"It's the rock Dottie gave me.
Remember?" he asked Dottie. "You said it
looked like Wisconsin."

"I didn't think you were listening," Dottie
said.

"I was," Leon said. "And you were right!
It is Wisconsin!"

"That's a cool rock," Victoria said.

"Leon has lots of cool rocks," Dottie said.

"Do you want to see his collection?" Casey asked.

"Can I?" Victoria asked her father.

"Sure," Hy said. "Maybe you can start a collection, too, after we move into our house."

Victoria beamed. She and her new friends started walking to Leon's house.

"Wait," Hy called. He hopped on his stilts and ran over. "Want to borrow these?" He stepped down and offered the stilts to Victoria.

She grabbed them. "Thanks, Dad!" She hopped up and starting walking.

Dottie, Casey, and Leon watched, amazed. They didn't know Victoria could walk on stilts, too!

"I'm going to start a club when I get to my new school," she told them as they walked. "I'm going to call it the Victoria Club. It's going to be for solving mysteries on stilts. And anyone who wants to be in it can join."

"Can you teach us to walk on stilts so we can join?" Casey asked.

"You can be the very first members," Victoria said.

Dottie smiled. She loved being first.

Back-to-School Memories from Students Like You!

Last September, the Lucky Book Club asked 2nd- and 3rd-grade students what their first day of school was like. Was their new classroom similar to the one they had last year? Was it fun to see their friends again? Did things go as they thought they would?

After hundreds of students just like you sent in their essays, five winners were selected. Now you can read all about their first day of school and see how it compares with yours!

The first day of school arrived. I was so excited that I was a third grader. In third grade you get to learn awesome things like computers, science, and cursive writing. My teacher is young and very nice. She wore black flip-flops. I knew that we would become fast buds.

This year I have a desk of my own, a student planner, a mailbox, and my teacher treats us like adults. My recess is on the older kids' playground. I look forward to doing fun and exciting projects. I feel like I am almost nine years old!

By Lilyanna S.
Grade: 3

My school got rebuilt this year, so I had not only a new classroom, but a whole new campus to get used to! My classroom was filled with all sorts of Indian things: tipis, real animal skins, and a huge dream catcher. My friends and I got to be a part of a "tribe" in our classroom. We are the Navajo. What my teacher didn't know was that I really loved Indian things even before I got into her room! So I know I am going to love my new classroom because it's already filled with lots of things that interest me and the learning has just begun!

By Tali U.
Grade: 2

This year will be the most exciting year ever! I used to have a tracheostomy, but it was taken out over the summer. When I had a tracheostomy, I had to go to school with a nurse who used to drive me to school. This year, I will be going to school by myself. The first day I felt great, and very independent, especially riding the school bus for the first time! My best friend, Timothy, told me he read all the Magic Tree House books over the summer and he challenged me to read them all too. I said sure, and started book number two. This year will be the most exciting year ever!

By Cameron M.
Grade: 2

This year when I went to 3rd grade I took a route that I've been going on since I was a baby. I call it "Memory Lane" because when my brothers were in school here I used to ride my tricycle or be pulled in a wagon to get them to school. Now my brothers are in Middle School. I am the only brother left here. When I walk, I still remember everything that happened going that route with my brothers.

By David F.
Grade: 3

The day I was back at school was very scary. All my new teachers were tall. Very tall indeed! I got scared looking at them. That first day all my friends were scared too. My friends and I all were scared of Mrs. Cathegan. She was our class teacher. The classroom was very different from the old one. The old one was very dirty. I didn't like our last teacher much (no offense!).

Even though the teachers were scary, no one else was. I was very happy until my milkshake fell on my uniform. I had to wear a senior's uniform because the senior was allowed to wear any type of dress he liked. I say that this is very unfair.

The day was fun and because I was known to be good that first day, our teacher gave me a lollipop which I gave to my sister because I don't like lollipops. Anyway, it was fun.

By Neeharika P.
Grade: 3

The Monthly Calendar

~~~~~~ Issue Five • Volume Five ~~~~~~

SEPTEMBER

Publisher: Casey Calendar
Editor: Dottie Plum
Fact Checker: Leon Spector

Calendar Club Saves School Carnival

The Fruitvale Back-to-School Carnival was always big news in September. But this September the news wasn't all good!

Calendar Club members Casey Calendar, Dottie Plum, and Leon Spector were upset to discover that carnival prizes and games were disappearing from their school! Someone was trying to ruin their carnival fun!

The Calendar Club quickly got on the case. They followed the clues and suspects. And what they found out was that things are sometimes not what they seem.

Thanks to the Calendar Club, the Fruitvale Back-to-School Carnival went on as planned. And this year it was more fun than ever!

DOTTIE'S WEATHER BOX

Autumn is coming! Two leaves on our maple tree have turned red. Three leaves on our oak tree have turned yellow. The evergreen tree is still all green.

How many leaves have changed color in all?

ASK LEON

Do you have a question about a state for Leon Spector? If you do, send it to him and he'll answer it for you.

Dear Leon,
Does Wisconsin have a state animal?
From,
I Love Animals

Dear I Love Animals,
Wisconsin has three state animals! The state wildlife animal is the white-tailed deer. The state domesticated animal is the cow. And the regular Wisconsin state animal is the badger. I'd say Wisconsinites love animals as much as you do!

Your friend,
Leon
P.S. Guess what? I love animals, too!